with love
for my mother and father
sister and brothers

Petrouchka

Adapted from Igor Stravinsky and Alexandre Benois
by ELIZABETH CLEAVER

ATHENEUM   1980   NEW YORK

LIBRARY OF CONGRESS CATALOGING IN PUBLICATION DATA

Cleaver, Elizabeth, date
Petrouchka.

SUMMARY: Retells the story of the ballet, in which a puppet with a soul
tries to win the love of a ballerina during a Shrovetide Fair.
[1. Folklore—Russia. 2. Ballets—Stories, plots, etc.
3. Puppets and puppet-plays—Fiction] I. Title.
PZ8.1.C54Pe   [398.2] [E]   79-14436
ISBN 0-689-30704-7

Published simultaneously in Canada by Macmillan of Canada
Printed by A. Hoen & Company, Baltimore, Maryland

Typography by M. M. Ahern
First Edition

It was wintertime. Crystal patterns of snow were fluttering and twirling in the air as if they were dancing.

Near the gate of the city, sleighs raced over the snow, jingling their bells and bringing the children to the Shrovetide Fair.

It was an exciting day. Children ran to see the carousel, the puppet theater, and the booths that sold gingerbread cookies and toys.

They watched an organ grinder begin to play; and everyone else came to listen, too. And to watch a girl with a triangle dance and pirouette to the music.

In another place a second dancer stepped out in competition with the first, and the crowd moved to see her.

Next a group of peasants began to dance to a Russian folk tune, and everyone turned to watch them.

Then suddenly, with a loud thrum, thrum, thrum, two drummers appeared on the puppet stage. The children shouted with delight as they saw a man in a high peaked hat poke his head through the curtain. The puppet master was about to begin his show.

He stepped in front of the curtain to play a magic song on his flute. The curtain flew back, and there hung three motionless puppets. On the left was a Moor. In the center was a ballerina. On the right was Petrouchka, a clown.

The puppet master sounded his flute again, three times, and immediately the puppets woke up and began to dance.

Soon everyone could see that the Moor and Petrouchka were enchanted by the ballerina, who danced delicately on her pointes.

As the Moor began to flirt with her, Petrouchka became very jealous. This made the puppet master very angry because this was not a part of the dance. He sounded his flute again, and once more the puppets became rigid and still.

The dance was over. The puppet master kicked Petrouchka into his bare, narrow room. Left alone, the poor puppet rose to his feet and tried to find a way out; but it was useless. The door was locked.

He thought of the ballerina and was filled with love. Overcome with despair and pain and loneliness, he danced to a sad music that came from within him.

Then all at once, in the midst of his sorrow, the door flew open. In came the ballerina herself, doing a teasing dance all around the room. Petrouchka was filled with delight and leaped awkwardly about the room to show his pleasure.

But the ballerina was disgusted by his dance. She thought he was behaving like a clown and left the room, slamming the door behind her. Petrouchka rushed to follow, only to find the door locked again. Once more he was alone and unhappy.

Inside his elegant room, next door to Petrouchka, the Moor lay on his couch, idly playing with a coconut. First he grasped it with his feet, then he twirled it in the air, and finally he let it fall as he heard a distant drumbeat. He glanced at the door and saw the ballerina come in carrying a toy trumpet.

The ballerina danced to the music she made herself on the trumpet, and found that she liked to please the Moor.

As for the Moor, he watched awhile and then decided to dance himself. The two waltzed around the room until a great pounding sound began to disturb them. And suddenly the jealous Petrouchka came through a hole he had knocked in the wall, because he thought the ballerina needed his help.

As he entered, he threw himself on the Moor. The Moor drew his scimitar and ran it at Petrouchka. Unprepared for this attack, Petrouchka went rushing out, and the Moor ran after him.

Outside, night had come to the fair. The puppet stage was dark and quiet, but there was still music and gaiety everywhere. Everyone was having a good time dancing.

Groups of masqueraders roamed the streets. Pairs of lovers danced in dark corners.

The children's nursemaids danced with the coachmen.

There was even a dancing bear, swaggering clumsily on his hind legs as he did a few tricks for his attendant. Everyone was so happy that no one heard anything but the music.

Until quite abruptly the music stopped. At that moment a terrible cry came from the puppet theater. The merrymakers stood horrified as Petrouchka ran through the street, trying to escape the Moor.

The Moor swung his scimitar. It whirred through the air and struck Petrouchka. With a heartbroken cry, the puppet fell dead. And the ballerina and the fairgoers simply looked on in stunned silence while the Moor hastily fled into the night.

The puppet master, who had heard Petrouchka's cry, now came hurrying into the street. Breaking into the crowd, he saw the fallen puppet.

Hastily, he lifted the straw-stuffed puppet, hoping he could repair the damage. But before he could do anything, a wild shriek came from the sky. Everyone looked up, and on the roof of the theater they saw the spirit of Petrouchka. The real Petrouchka was free at last.

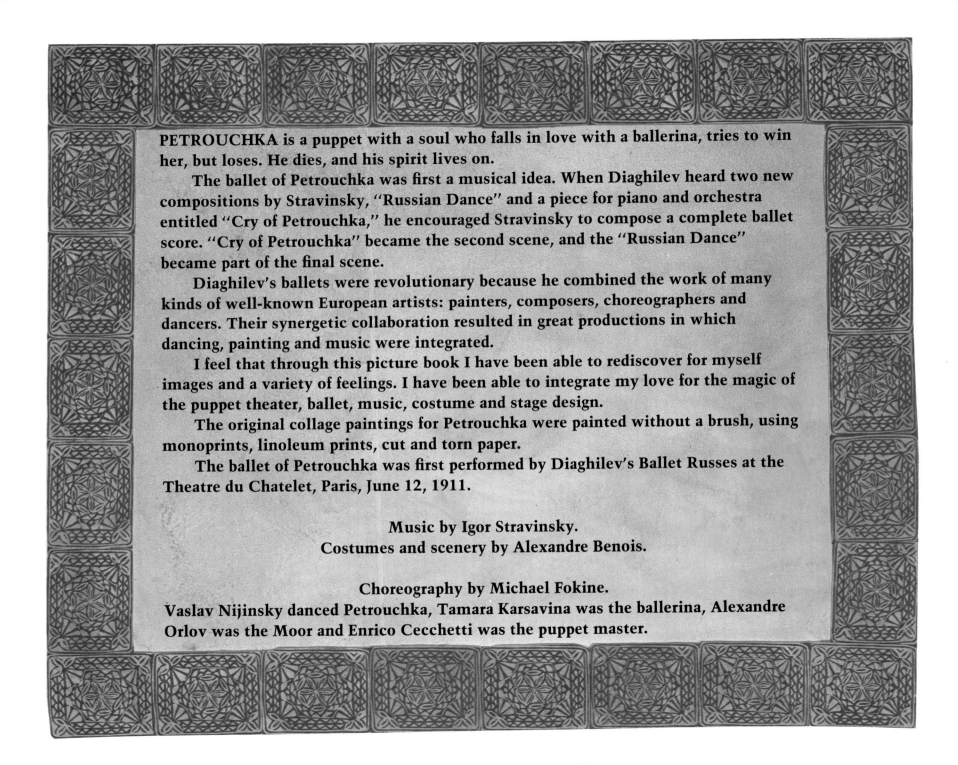

PETROUCHKA is a puppet with a soul who falls in love with a ballerina, tries to win her, but loses. He dies, and his spirit lives on.

The ballet of Petrouchka was first a musical idea. When Diaghilev heard two new compositions by Stravinsky, "Russian Dance" and a piece for piano and orchestra entitled "Cry of Petrouchka," he encouraged Stravinsky to compose a complete ballet score. "Cry of Petrouchka" became the second scene, and the "Russian Dance" became part of the final scene.

Diaghilev's ballets were revolutionary because he combined the work of many kinds of well-known European artists: painters, composers, choreographers and dancers. Their synergetic collaboration resulted in great productions in which dancing, painting and music were integrated.

I feel that through this picture book I have been able to rediscover for myself images and a variety of feelings. I have been able to integrate my love for the magic of the puppet theater, ballet, music, costume and stage design.

The original collage paintings for Petrouchka were painted without a brush, using monoprints, linoleum prints, cut and torn paper.

The ballet of Petrouchka was first performed by Diaghilev's Ballet Russes at the Theatre du Chatelet, Paris, June 12, 1911.

Music by Igor Stravinsky.
Costumes and scenery by Alexandre Benois.

Choreography by Michael Fokine.
Vaslav Nijinsky danced Petrouchka, Tamara Karsavina was the ballerina, Alexandre Orlov was the Moor and Enrico Cecchetti was the puppet master.